Animals
on the Farm

Vicki Coghill

illustrated by
Stephen Michael King

ISBN 0-439-20841-6

Copyright © 1999 by Scholastic Australia Pty Limited.
All rights reserved. Published by Scholastic Inc., 555 Broadway, New York, NY 10012,
by arrangement with Scholastic Australia Pty Limited.
SCHOLASTIC and associated logos are trademarks and/or registered trademarks of Scholastic Inc.

12 11 10 9 8 7 6 5   3 4 5/0
Printed in the U.S.A.   08
First Scholastic printing, September 2000
Designed by Trish Hayes
Edited by Julian Gray

SCHOLASTIC INC.
New York   Toronto   London   Auckland   Sydney
Mexico City   New Delhi   Hong Kong

One day all the animals got out.

Dad went to get the cows.
He ran and ran but the cows got away.

Dad went to get the sheep.
He ran and ran but the sheep got away.

Dad went to get the pigs.
He ran and ran but the pigs got away.

Dad went to get the horses.
He ran and ran but the horses got away.

Dad went to get the dog.

The dog ran and ran and *no-one* got away.